The Easter Bunny That Overslept

By Priscilla and Otto Friedrich

Illustrated by Donald Saaf

HarperCollins Publishers

The Easter Bunny That Overslept was first published in 1957 by Otto and Priscilla Friedrich, with illustrations by Adrienne Adams. In 1983, Adrienne Adams reillustrated this tale, which was revised with the authors' approval for a modern audience. For this newest edition, with art by Donald Saaf, the text has once again been revised for a new generation, with the approval and permission of Otto and Priscilla Friedrich's estate.

The Easter Bunny That Overslept

Text copyright © 2002 by the Estate of Otto and Priscilla Friedrich

Illustrations copyright © 2002 by Donald Saaf

Printed in the U.S.A. All rights reserved.

www.harperchildrens.com

Library of Congress Cataloging-in-Publication Data

Friedrich, Priscilla.

The Easter bunny that overslept / by Priscilla and Otto Friedrich ; illustrated by
Donald Saaf.–[Rev. ed.].

p.   cm.

Summary: Having slept past Easter, the Easter bunny tries to distribute his eggs on
Mother's Day, the Fourth of July, and Halloween, but no one is interested until finally
Santa Claus is able to get him back on track.

ISBN 0-06-029645-3 – ISBN 0-06-029646-1 (lib. bdg.)

[1. Tardiness–Fiction. 2. Easter–Fiction. 3. Rabbits–Fiction. 4. Christmas–Fiction.]

I. Friedrich, Otto, 1929– II. Saaf, Donald, ill. III. Title.

PZ7.F9152 Eas 2002

[E]–dc21   00-049879

CIP

AC

Typography by Stephanie Bart-Horvath

1 2 3 4 5 6 7 8 9 10

❖

Revised Edition

To the memory of Tony —M.F.

For Isak, Olaf, and Anna —D.S.

THE EASTER BUNNY was sound asleep, dreaming of a sunny day when he would bring painted eggs to all the children. But it was Easter Day, and it was raining. Snug in his bed, the bunny slept on. The children woke up excited, but there were no eggs to find, only the jelly beans that their parents had bought.

That month it rained every day; then in May the sun came out. The bunny woke up. Yawn! Stretch! Quickly he put on his Easter clothes and hopped and sang all the way to the first house.

"My eggs are blue,
Red and green, too.
A pink one for you
All nice and new—
Hoppity Happity Easter to you!"

A family sat in their garden eating a big pink cake.
The Easter Bunny proudly offered them his basket
of eggs.

"What's this?" exclaimed the father.

"Why, it's the Easter Bunny," said the little girl.

The mother shook her head. "Easter was weeks ago."

"Today is Mother's Day," the boy added.

Then the baby said the only words he knew: "Bye-bye. Bye-bye."

Poor Easter Bunny! He tried other houses, but no one wanted his eggs, and some people even scolded him for not being on time.

The little bunny sadly returned to his home. It seemed forever till next Easter. After May came June, after June came July, and—
Why, I'll be a Fourth of July Bunny! he thought.

He made himself a spectacular hat and repainted his eggs—red, white, and blue, with stars and stripes.

On the Fourth of July he hopped to town, where everyone was watching a parade.

What a parade! Trumpets and trombones! Flags and floats! Soldiers, Boy Scouts, and Girl Scouts marched. And hopping along to their drumbeat was the Fourth of July Bunny with his basket of eggs.

"Stop the parade!" the mayor shouted. "Who are you?"

The rabbit felt shy. "Well, I'm really the Easter Bunny," he said in a tiny voice. "But I overslept and missed Easter." Then he held up his basket of eggs.

"Happy Fourth of July, everybody!"

"The Fourth of July is no time for eggs," the mayor said crossly. "Now go away!"

The parade marched on, and the children followed, forgetting all about the Easter Bunny. He was left alone.

He tried knocking on doors, offering his painted eggs, but everyone thought he was joking.

Far away, crowds cheered as firecrackers boomed. Rockets zoomed into the sky and turned into clusters of stars.

The Easter Bunny hopped sadly back home and fell asleep again.

Summer passed. Autumn came, and the leaves blew
down from the trees. Still the bunny slept.

One spooky night when the wind was howling,
the bunny heard a knock at his door.

Three little ghosts stood outside.

"Trick or treat!" they shouted, for it was Halloween.

"Wait right there," the bunny cried happily, and hopped inside to get his Easter eggs.

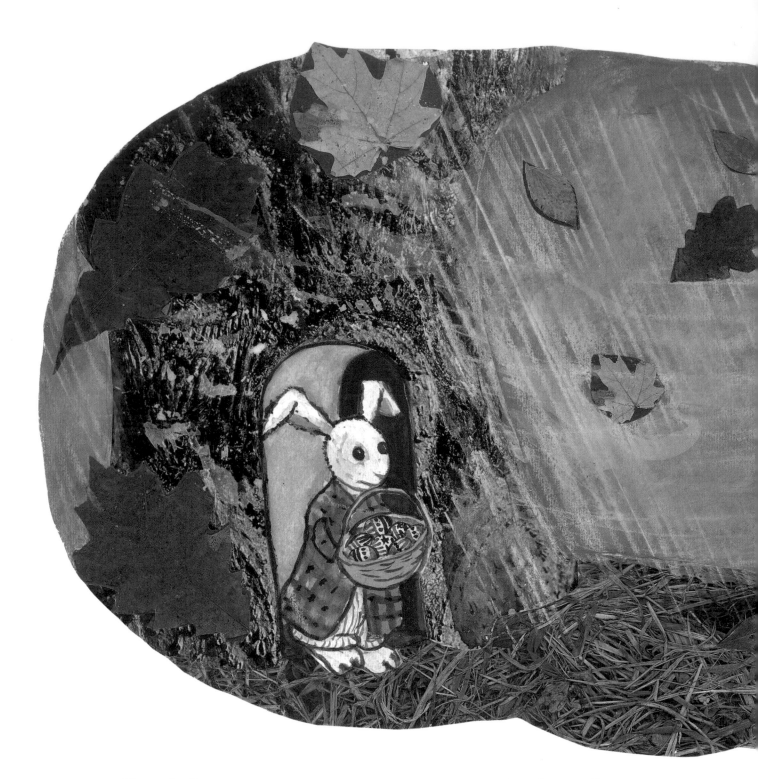

The children were surprised to see a basket of eggs.

"What are those?" they asked.

"Easter eggs. I mean Fourth of July eggs. I mean—"
The little bunny sighed and hung his head. Why
bother to explain? No one wanted his eggs.

He looked so sad that the children didn't play a trick
on him. They just ran away laughing and shouting,
"Easter eggs on Halloween! Who ever heard of such
a thing?"

The Easter Bunny stood in his doorway, shivering in the wind. He waited for other children to come, but they didn't. Suddenly, a fierce gale swept the

little rabbit off his feet and carried him high up in
the air.

He landed a long way away.

At first all he could see was snow. Then he read a sign, SANTA'S HOUSE, and followed its arrow, hopping down a path between rows of Christmas trees. At Santa's door he knocked very timidly.

"Well, bless my soul!" Santa said, when he saw the bunny. "Come in! Come in!"

The little rabbit told Santa everything that had happened since he had overslept on Easter.

"Well, now," said Santa, "there is nothing we can do about your Easter eggs, of course. But if you want to make the children happy, I have plenty of work for you."

The bunny painted toys—dolls and drums, airplanes
and elephants, and tops like spinning color wheels.

He had such a good time he forgot all about the eggs that nobody wanted.

On Christmas Eve Santa loaded his sleigh and asked the Easter Bunny to come along. Off they flew. Some of the rooftops where they landed had narrow chimneys. The Easter Bunny would take the toys from

Santa's sack and slide down the chimneys easily. Each time, Santa marveled. "I never could hop up and down those chimneys as fast as that!" Then the reindeer flew on to the next house.

After all the presents had been delivered, they returned to Santa's for cookies and hot chocolate. The Easter Bunny was growing tired and wanted to go home to his snug little bed.

"Wait," Santa said. "I have a gift for you, too." Inside the box was a gold alarm clock.

"Oh, thank you, thank you, Santa. I'll set it to go off Easter Sunday."

Months later, when the alarm clock rang, the Easter Bunny jumped up and filled *two baskets of eggs.*

He hopped to the first house. The baby who could
say only "Bye-bye" knew more words now.

"Hi, Easter Bunny!" he called, and took an egg.
"Happy Easter," the bunny said gaily.

That spring everyone wanted his beautiful eggs.
And because of the gold alarm clock, the Easter
Bunny was never late again.